Beautifully Me

For all the kids who are learning what "beautiful" truly means.
I hope the pages ahead help you in your journey of celebrating yourself.
I wish I'd had a story like this when I was a young brown girl
discovering myself and the world. So this book is not just for you,
dear reader—it's also for a younger me.

—N. N.

To the Zitouni family, for all your warmth and love

—N. H. A.

Beautifully Me

Written by
NABELA NOOR

Illustrated by NABI H. ALI

Simon & Schuster Books for Young Readers
New York   London   Toronto   Sydney   New Delhi

Salaam! My name is Zubi Chowdhury.
Yesterday, I woke up before the sun.
I knew it was going to be a special day.
It was my first day of school!

I put on my blue overalls and pink shirt with the fancy puffy sleeves. Amma had it made just for me in Bangladesh. I twisted my hair into two pigtails with my lucky butterfly clips and slid on my bangles.

I ran to my parents' room to show them my first-day outfit. Baba was helping Amma wrap her yellow sari around her body. She looked so beautiful—like sunshine and mango lassis.

"Oof!" Amma said. "Look at this tummy—I'm getting too big!"

Why was Amma so sad?

"Good morning, Dadi Ma!"

"Shubho shokal, Zubi," Dadi Ma corrected. "Remember to practice your Bangla."

My big sister, Naya, buzzed into the kitchen like a busy bee.

"Can I have oatmeal instead, Dadi Ma?"

Oatmeal?

Naya hates oatmeal!

"Why don't you want the parathas I made for you?" Dadi Ma asked.

My tummy cheered as I smelled the flaky, buttery bread in front of me. How could she say no to parathas?

Naya shrugged. "I'm on a diet. I want to lose weight so I can look pretty in time for the school dance."

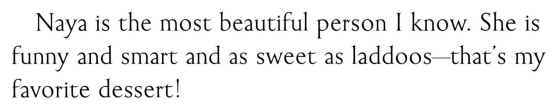

Naya is the most beautiful person I know. She is funny and smart and as sweet as laddoos—that's my favorite dessert!

Why would she say she's not pretty?

I want to look good for my first day of school. Should *I* go on a diet too?

Baba popped his head into the
kitchen and jingled his keys.
"Girls, let's get going!"

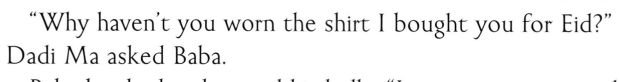

"Why haven't you worn the shirt I bought you for Eid?"
Dadi Ma asked Baba.
    Baba laughed and patted his belly. "I put on some pounds,
Ma. I am up to a large now. Not good."

Why was a large *not good?*

I grabbed my backpack,

gave my kitten,
Kulfi, a big kiss,

and rushed out the door.

My teacher is amazing!

We did crafts, learned new songs, and took a tour of the library—all before lunchtime.

I even made a new friend! Her name is Kareema.

At recess, some kids hop like bunnies.
Some kids run faster than race cars.
Some kids climb all the way to the sun.

"Alix, you look fat in that dress!"

Alix looks beautiful in their silk dress. It shines like the sun! But Kennedy doesn't sound like she's giving a compliment.

Why is looking fat bad?

Do *I* look fat in my overalls?

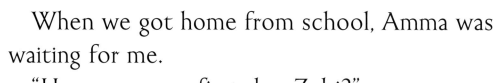

When we got home from school, Amma was
waiting for me.
"How was your first day, Zubi?"
I thought about what happened during recess.
"Uh . . . it was fine."

Amma spent the rest of the afternoon cooking.
Dadi Ma helped by chopping onions and vegetables.
The house smelled delicious!

When we sat down for dinner, I was so excited to eat the khabar.
"No rice for me, thanks, Amma," Naya said.
No rice? Naya loves rice!
Oh yeah, I forgot.
Naya was on a diet.

I thought about large not being good. I thought about Amma, Naya, and Alix.

If they are not beautiful . . . how could I be?

Maybe I need to change too.

"Zubi jaan, don't you want any rice and chicken? It's your favorite," Amma said.

"I'm on a diet."

"A diet?" Amma looked confused. "Zubi, you shouldn't be on a diet."

"Naya said you have to be on a diet to be pretty," I said. "And I want to be pretty."

"Why would you think that, Zubi? You are beautiful!"

"But you told Baba your tummy was too big, and you were sad. And Baba said large is not good! Then, at recess, Kennedy teased Alix for looking fat in their dress. I don't want kids to make fun of me, too!"

I ran to my room and shut the door. My heart felt like it was crying. Maybe it wasn't a special day like I'd thought.

"Zubi," Baba said, "sometimes when people are feeling sad or hurting inside, they try to make other people feel the same way. That might be why Kennedy was mean to your friend."

I never thought about why someone would be mean before. "But sometimes we can be mean to ourselves without even realizing it. And when we hurt ourselves, we hurt the people we love and who love us. That's what we did to you today, and we're sorry."

"Yes," Amma said. "You saw me being unkind to my tummy. But I'm grateful for my belly—after all, it helped me carry you and bring you into the world."

"I'm sorry too," said Naya. "It's hard not to compare myself to other people. But I'd rather be me—your sister—than anybody else."

"Do you know why we named you Zubi?" Amma asked.

I shook my head and sniffled.

"We named you Zubi because it means 'loving and understanding.' And we knew you would make the world more beautiful just by being Zubi."

"I don't even know what 'beautiful' means anymore," I admitted.

"You get to define what is beautiful. Whatever your body looks like, beauty is how you make people feel and the kind things you do. A beautiful person is someone who embraces who they are and helps others do the same. There is only one Zubi, and that makes you beautifully you."

"I can make the world
more beautiful?"
"Yes, Zubi jaan."

"Then you all are beautiful!" I told Amma and Naya and Baba.
"Just the way you are."

I gave them a big, big hug.

"Thank you for reminding us of that," Naya whispered to me.

Later, Amma tucked me into bed and kissed me good night.
Through the window, the moon and the stars smiled down
at me. Everything was beautiful.
It was a special day after all.

My name is Zubi, and that means "loving and understanding." I am one of a kind, and that makes me beautifully me. There is only one you, and that makes you beautifully you.

Today is my second day of school, and I am on a mission to make the world a bit more Zubi.

GLOSSARY

Eid: the festive holiday that ends the month-long Muslim observance of Ramadan

jaan: a term of endearment; "darling" or "dear"

khabar: "food" in Bengali

kulfi: a frozen dairy dessert

laddoo: a ball-shaped dessert made with flour, milk, butter, and sugar

lassi: a popular yogurt-based drink typically made with fruit and spices

Salaam: a respectful greeting in many Arabic-speaking and Muslim communities

sari: a traditional South Asian garment that wearers wrap around their waist and drape over their shoulder

shubho shokal: "good morning" in Bengali

paratha: a flaky, layered flatbread

ACKNOWLEDGMENTS

I would like to thank my parents, for not only believing in me but for leaving their home, their land, and their families for their children to have a shot at the American Dream. I will never be able to repay you both for your sacrifices, but I pray that sharing a glimpse into our culture, customs, and language through Zubi's lens makes you proud.

This book would not be possible without my manager, Kyle Santillo; the entire Scale Management team; my agents, Jade Sherman & Marienor Madrilejo; the entire A3 team; my attorney, Ashley Silver; and my business managers, Melissa Morton and Elle Dalconzo. Thank you for every call, every meeting, and for taking a chance on this little brown girl from a small town in Pennsylvania. I am forever grateful for each and every one of you.

Thank you to Simon Green for believing in *Beautifully Me* with enthusiasm and relentless optimism, and to Kendra Levin for being the best editor imaginable. Your faith in my writing gave me the confidence I needed to bring this book to life. And thank you to Laurent Linn and Nabi Ali for transforming my words into a beautiful, vibrant world through art that will be imprinted in my heart forever.

Thank you to my brothers and sisters—Amin bhaia, Bithi Appu, Tushar bhaia, Mohtaz, and Neharika—for being my best friends, biggest cheerleaders, and strongest influences. It is the honor of my life to be your sister.

Thank you to my nieces and nephews—Inaya, Aaliyah, Kadin, Eshan, Lylah, and Zayn—for being a massive inspiration for this book. I want you to grow in a world that reminds you of your individual beauty. You all make Zubi who she is. Thank you for making me the proudest Moni Ma.

And to my husband, Seth. Thank you for being by my side through every draft. Every written word. Every spark and every idea. You believed in this book before it even became a reality, just like you always do whenever I dare to dream. Thank you for giving me wings.

And to my future baby. Whenever you're ready, wherever you are. This book would not be possible if I weren't thinking of you through every second and every word.

I love you with all of my heart.

—*Nabela Noor*